The Mystery of
The Flyaway Balloon

Collins

An imprint of HarperCollins*Publishers*

It was the day of the Toy Town Summer Fete.
Noddy was to help Martha Monkey with the big,
red hot-air balloon.

Martha explained what they had to do. "Everyone has to pay six coins and then they climb into the basket. We undo two loops of the rope and the balloon goes up into the air. Don't untie *three* loops of rope or the balloon will fly away."

"You have the first go," suggested Noddy.
He untied two loops of the rope. Up, up, up went
the balloon, with Martha laughing and waving from
the basket!

"Look, Gobbo and Sly are hiding behind that tree," shouted Martha, "and I can see Miss Pink Cat over there!"

Noddy couldn't wait for his turn! He had just pulled the balloon back down and secured the rope when Miss Pink Cat arrived. "You shouldn't be *playing* with the balloon!" she said crossly.

So Noddy didn't have his turn in the balloon, instead he and Martha started work at once. They painted a sign saying, 'Balloon Rides'.

Then they made another sign saying, 'Queue Here'. All around them the other toys were working hard too.

Tessie Bear and Dinah Doll had made lots of delicious cakes and buns for the cake stall.

Jumbo set up the ice-cream stall and Mr Sparks made a huge sign with 'Toy Town Summer Fete' written on it.

TOY TOWN SUMMER FETE

Miss Pink Cat was the Very Important Person who had been asked to officially open the fete at two o'clock.

"Is everything ready?" she asked haughtily.

"There's one thing missing," said Noddy. "We need to help people climb up into the basket. Not everyone can climb as well as Martha! I've got some steps at home but I'll need Martha's help to carry them."

"Clockwork Mouse, will you look after the hot-air balloon for a few minutes?" asked Noddy.

"Of course," said Clockwork Mouse, helpfully.

Noddy and Martha drove off to collect the steps.

Suddenly, Sly appeared by the hot-air balloon. Sly and Gobbo, the two goblins, had been watching Noddy and Martha all morning.

"Hello Clockwork Mouse," said Sly. "Oh look, isn't that a coin on the ground?"

Clockwork Mouse squealed with delight and ran towards the coin. In a flash, Gobbo appeared from behind the basket where he had been hiding. He climbed into the basket and Sly undid the rope!

One, two, *three* loops were untied and the balloon floated up into the sky.

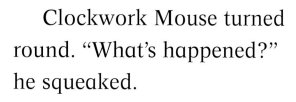

Clockwork Mouse turned round. "What's happened?" he squeaked.

"Gosh, you really should have been more careful," said Sly, as the balloon floated up into the sky.

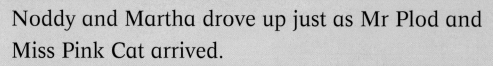

Noddy and Martha drove up just as Mr Plod and
Miss Pink Cat arrived.

"What has happened to the balloon?" cried
Miss Pink Cat. Noddy noticed Sly hanging around.

"Sly, what are you up to?" asked Noddy, suspiciously.

"It wasn't me," said Sly. "Look, the balloon's up there and I'm still here!"

Noddy noticed goblin footprints next to the balloon sign but there was no time to argue.

"Quick, Martha! Jump in!" said Noddy, getting in his car. "We'll follow it!"

Martha and Noddy drove off, past the pond, past the ice cream parlour, past Tessie Bear's house, but it was no good. The balloon was going too fast.

Noddy was sure he saw a goblin hand reaching up out of the basket just as the balloon drifted out of sight.

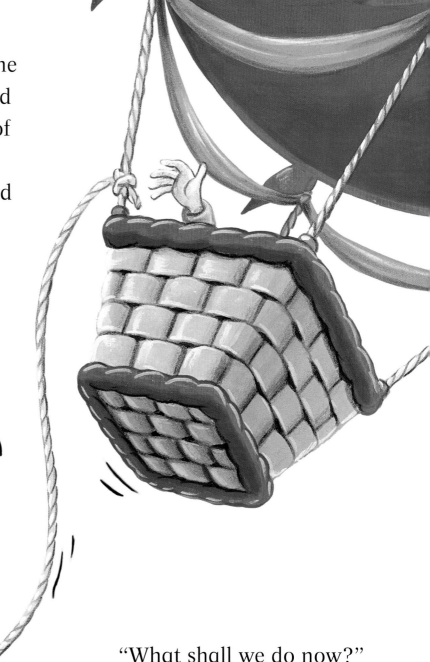

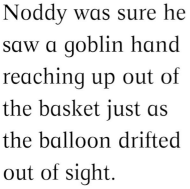

"What shall we do now?" asked Martha.

"Let's go and see Big-Ears," said Noddy.

Gobbo chuckled as he secretly steered the balloon towards Dark Wood. He had agreed to meet Sly there just before two o'clock.

"This is easy," said Gobbo to himself as he tried to land the balloon. But landing was a bit harder than Gobbo realised. On his way down, he missed his landing spot and got stuck in a tree!

"Oh, no," wailed Gobbo. "I'm stuck! What shall I do now?"

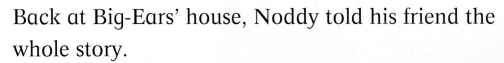

Back at Big-Ears' house, Noddy told his friend the whole story.

"There were *two* sets of goblin footprints at the balloon stand," said Noddy, "and I'm sure I saw a goblin hand just as the balloon drifted away."

"But it couldn't have been Sly," said Big-Ears, scratching his head.

"But where was Gobbo?" cried Noddy, jumping up. "Come on, Martha. I think I know where we can find the flyaway balloon!"

Noddy and Martha drove to Dark Wood. It was almost two o'clock. And what did they find? An unhappy Gobbo, in a balloon, stuck at the top of a tree. And Sly, looking cross, at the bottom of the tree.

Martha quickly climbed to the top of the tree and brought the balloon's rope down to Noddy who tied it to his car. Martha climbed into the basket to help steer the balloon down safely.

"You're coming with us," said Noddy to Gobbo as sternly as he could.

The Toy Town clock was just striking two o'clock as Noddy, Martha, the flyaway balloon and the two goblins arrived.

"We've found the flyaway balloon!" announced Noddy and he told everyone what had happened. Mr Plod arrested Gobbo and Sly immediately.

"I declare the Toy Town Fete open," said
Miss Pink Cat in a very posh voice.

But no-one heard her. They were too busy cheering
Noddy for solving the mystery of the flyaway balloon.

Here are some more books for you to enjoy:

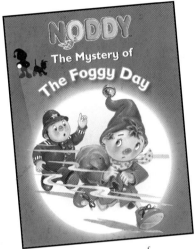

The Mystery of
The Foggy Day
ISBN 0-00712360-4

The Mystery of
The Stolen Bicycles
ISBN 0-00712361-2

The Mystery of
The Missing Friends
ISBN 0-00712358-2

For further information please contact www.NODDY.com

This edition first published in Great Britain by HarperCollins Publishers Ltd in 2002

1 3 5 7 9 10 8 6 4 2

Copyright © 2002 Enid Blyton Ltd. Enid Blyton's signature mark and the words "NODDY" and "TOYLAND" are Registered Trade Marks of Enid Blyton Ltd.
For further information on Enid Blyton please contact www.blyton.com

ISBN: 0 00712359 0

Reproduction by Graphic Studio S.r.l. Verona
Printed in China by Jade Productions